www.hollywebbanimalstories.com

STRIPES PUBLISHING
An imprint of the Little Tiger Group
1 Coda Studios, 189 Munster Road,
London SW6 6AW

This hardback edition first published
in Great Britain in 2017

Text copyright © Holly Webb, 2017
Illustrations copyright © Artful Doodlers, 2017
Cover illustration copyright © Simon Mendez, 2017
Author photograph copyright © Nigel Bird

ISBN: 978-1-84715-793-5

A CIP catalogue record for this book is available
from the British Library.

Printed and bound in the UK.

2 4 6 8 10 9 7 5 3 1

THE
STORM
DOG

HOLLY WEBB

stripes

For Jamie

~ HOLLY WEBB

For George and Barbara

~ JO

CHAPTER
ONE

Tilly sat at the end of the sofa, looking worriedly at her mum. She was trying to go back through her day at school, wondering if she'd done anything wrong without realizing it that would have made her teacher call home, She couldn't think why else Mum would want to have "a talk" with her just when she'd got back from school.

"You know we're going to Grandma Ellen's house for Christmas?" her mum began slowly.

"Yes! Oh – can't we go?" Tilly slumped a little. "There's nothing wrong with Grandma, is there? Or Great-Gran?" she added, her eyes widening. Great-Gran *was* nearly ninety, even though she was one of the most energetic people Tilly had ever met. She and Tilly's grandma shared a cottage together, and Great-Gran even did most of the gardening.

"Don't panic! It's all fine – we're still going." Mum patted her knee and then sighed. "It's just that there's so much happening at work, I'm not going to be able to take as much time off as I'd planned. I won't be able to go until the day before Christmas Eve."

Tilly made a face. They'd planned to be at Grandma's for a few days before Christmas and she'd been really looking forward to it. There seemed to be more Christmassy things to do there. If they didn't go till the twenty-third, Grandma would have already put up her Christmas tree and Tilly wouldn't get to help decorate it. They only had space for a tiny little tree in their flat and you could hardly fit any decorations on it at all. Maybe Grandma would even put the icing on the Christmas cake without her, too…

"That's ages away," she muttered.

Her mum sighed again. "I know. So, I spoke to Grandma earlier on and we were thinking – what if you went up on the train before me?"

"You mean go to Grandma's on my own?" Tilly stared at her mum. She'd never even considered *that*. She'd thought that Mum would say she had to go to holiday club at school again. She'd been just about to moan that holiday club was boring and now Mum had sprung a total surprise on her instead.

"Not for the whole time," her mum hurried to explain. "I'd be coming as soon as I can get off work. I know you love spending time with Grandma Ellen and Great-Gran."

"I do – I mean, I do want to. It's just that I've never been on a train on my own before." Tilly nibbled her bottom lip. Her grandma lived a long way away, in a village close to the Welsh border. It was at least an hour's journey by train. More like an hour and a half.

Her mum nodded. "I know – that's the bit that worries me, too, Tilly. I mean, I would put you on the train here and Grandma would meet you at the other end but it's still a big thing to do on your own. No… You're right, it's not going to work. I'll call Grandma later and tell her." She smiled at Tilly. "Don't worry! We'll still get to stay with them for most of Christmas."

Tilly leaned against her mum's shoulder. Could she do it? She went to school on her own now but that was different, it was only a ten-minute walk. She'd been really nervous the first time she did it, though. Perhaps she was making too much fuss about the train? "Don't call Grandma Ellen just yet," she murmured. "I'll … think about it."

"OK. But honestly, Tilly, I don't want you worrying about it." Mum eyed her thoughtfully. "So, did anything interesting happen at school today?"

Tilly sighed heavily. "Guess what Mrs Cole's done." She sat up again, folding her arms and glaring at her mum.

"Um… Given you loads of homework?"

"Worse than that! She's given us a project. To do in the Christmas holidays! It's not fair." Tilly slumped back against the sofa cushions. She'd thought maybe they'd get some spellings over the holidays, or a bit of maths. Not a great big project to do. Everyone in her class was complaining about it.

"What's it on?" Mum asked. "Something interesting?"

"The Second World War." Tilly peered

over at her. "We have to choose a topic, like rationing or something. I suppose it's sort of interesting."

"Oh, it definitely is!" Mum brightened up, tapping her fingers on the sofa as she thought. "You could make some of those weird wartime recipes – I bet we could find them online. Even some Christmassy ones. I'm sure there was a recipe for Christmas pudding with gravy powder in it…"

"Why would I want to make that? It sounds disgusting!" Tilly scrunched up her nose, frowning. "Why would they even *do* that?"

"To make it look the right colour, I think. Because they couldn't get most of the proper ingredients. But you should ask Great-Gran. Actually, Tilly, you could interview her for your project!

You're lucky, I shouldn't think many people in your class have someone in the family to ask."

"I suppose," Tilly agreed doubtfully. She sort of knew that Great-Gran had been a child during the war but she'd never sat down and asked her about it. "Would she mind?"

"I expect she'd love to tell you. We can ask her later when we phone."

Tilly nodded. "I'd better go and do my homework. I'll think about the train, OK?"

Grandma Ellen called Mum anyway, it turned out, just as they were cooking dinner. Tilly stirred the pasta sauce, listening to Mum's half of the conversation.

"Yes, I know. I'd mentioned maybe you could meet her at the station but Tilly's never been on a train on her own before. She's not sure… I'm sorry, we really wanted to come for longer. Oh, OK." Mum waved at Tilly. "Grandma wants to talk to you."

Tilly took the phone. "Hi, Grandma."

"Hello, Tilly love. Don't worry about

the train, we'll work something out. I could come and get you in the car."

Tilly saw Mum start to look worried – she was standing next to Tilly and she could hear Grandma, too. "You don't like driving long journeys," she reminded Grandma. "Oh, Mum's waving at me, she wants to talk to you again." Tilly went back to stirring the pasta sauce, hoping that Mum and Grandma wouldn't talk for too much longer. She was getting really hungry. After a few minutes, though, Mum handed her the phone again.

"Tilly." Her great-gran's voice sounded a little quavery but happy and Tilly smiled to hear her. "Hello, Great-Gran!" She could hear a snuffling noise on the other end of the line and for a moment she wondered if Great-Gran had a cold

– but then she realized. "Great-Gran, is that Tarran? Is he licking the phone?"

Tarran was Great-Gran's beautiful black-and-white sheepdog.

"No!" Her great-gran laughed. "But he's trying to. You know how nosy he is. Oh, Tilly, it's going to be wonderful to see you. It seems so long since you've visited."

"It is," Tilly agreed. "Great-Gran, can I ask you a favour? I've got a school project I have to do over the holidays, about the Second World War. I'd sort of forgotten that you were, um, in it. Can I ask you questions about it while I'm staying?"

Her great-gran laughed. "Of course you can, you silly thing. But I was only small then, Tilly. I didn't understand a lot of what was happening. In fact..." There was a pause, as if Great-Gran was thinking. "When the war broke out, I must have been almost exactly the same age as you."

"It doesn't have to be about battles and things," Tilly explained. "Mrs Cole said she wanted us to try and find out what life was like. Mum was talking about rationing."

"Oh, well, then you can ask me whatever you like, Tilly. I'll do my best. It was a very odd time, though, you know – we had to get used to a new place to live. That was so strange, sometimes we almost forgot we were there because of the war..."

"A new place?" Tilly asked.

"Don't you know, Tilly?" Great-Gran sounded surprised. "Haven't I ever told you? That's why we live here now, your grandma and I. Maybe I haven't... I came here on the train, lovey, just like you're going to, two days before the war broke out."

Tilly blinked in shock. She'd never realized. "You were an evacuee?"

Mrs Cole had shown them photographs of children who'd been evacuated at the beginning of the war. The government had expected that the big cities would be bombed, so children had been sent to the countryside to be safe. The strange thing about the photos was that even though the clothes were old-fashioned, most of the children looked like people she saw every day at school. It was weird to think that the war had happened to children, too – to a girl her own age, like Great-Gran had been. It felt like it should be a grown-up thing.

"You were really the same age as me, back then?" she murmured.

"Yes. I'm your ancient old great-grandma, remember? I was ten when the war started."

"So you were born in 1929... Wait a minute. If you got evacuated to Linchurch, where did you live before? Do you mean you never went back home?" Tilly's voice went squeaky with horror.

"Oh no, I did eventually, lovey, don't be upset. We were from Birmingham and we did go home, my brothers and me. But I never forgot those years in the country. I loved it. Birmingham never felt the same to me after. I went back to stay at the farm whenever I could, and then I met your great-grandad and that was that."

Tilly giggled. She couldn't imagine Great-Gran falling in love. She'd never known her great-grandad and Great-Gran had been old forever, or that's what it felt like. "I can't imagine you my age, Great-Gran."

"To be honest, Tilly, I looked quite like you. I had hair just the same colour as yours, except it was a bit shorter, I think. Yes, I'm sure that's right – I was ten when we left, Alfie was seven and little Eddie was five."

"Five!" Tilly sucked in a breath. That sounded so young to go away.

"I had to look after them both, my mum told me. I was so worried about them."

"It must have been scary." Tilly swallowed hard, feeling a little embarrassed. Gran and her brothers wouldn't have known where they were going, not from the way Mrs Cole had described the evacuees. They didn't know who they'd be living with when they got to the end of their journey. So why was she worrying about Mum putting her on a train at one station and Grandma meeting her at another? And if she went on the train, there'd be so much more time to spend with Grandma and Great-Gran.

She'd tell Mum she'd go, Tilly decided.

Great-Gran made a thoughtful *mmm* sort of noise. "Yes... Yes, I suppose it was scary... Oh, is that your timer going off, Tilly? Are you about to have dinner?"

Tilly had almost forgotten that she was starving. "Yes. Sorry, Great-Gran, I'd better go. But have you got any photos of you back then? Will you show them to me?"

"I'll dig them out for you," her great-gran promised. "And I've some of the letters my mother and father sent us as well. They must be up in the attic somewhere. See you soon, Tilly!"

CHAPTER
TWO

Tilly almost missed goodbye. She'd been expecting a jolt, slamming doors, maybe even someone blowing a whistle. But instead the station started to glide away – almost as if it was the benches and signs and people that were moving, not the train at all.

She pressed her nose against the glass, trying to see her mum waving on the platform. Part of her wanted to yell, *Stop!* But she squashed that bit down, and tried to smile and wave back. In just an hour and a half she'd be with Grandma and everything would be fine. It wasn't as if she was going that far, really. But it didn't stop the lurch of panic as the train gathered pace and drew out of the station. *Lots of people my age go to school by train every day*, Tilly told herself.

She couldn't see Mum at all now. Tilly sat back in her seat, clutching tightly at her backpack. She had a colouring book and pens in there, and a drink and a sandwich. At the last minute Mum had got her a book of puzzles in the shop at the station, too. Thinking about it, Mum had probably fussed so much because she was just as worried about Tilly going on the train on her own as Tilly was.

Tilly nodded at her reflection in the train window, remembering her talk with Great-Gran. At least she didn't have to look after anybody but herself. This was an adventure and not even a very scary one. Tilly glanced around the carriage. The train wasn't very full but there were a few other people scattered about. Most of them were getting books or magazines out of their bags or listening to music.

Tilly unzipped her backpack and found the parcel that she had packed in there that morning. Great-Gran had sent it, Mum explained. Written under the address in Great-Gran's thin, delicate handwriting were the words: *Not to be opened until you're on the train.* Mum had shown it to her at breakfast. It was very clever of Great-Gran and Mum, Tilly realized now. It had stopped her being nervous, just when she'd been feeling panicky and like she didn't really want to eat anything.

It was an old-fashioned sort of parcel, Tilly decided. It wasn't in a padded envelope, the way Mum sent presents to Tilly's cousins, but wrapped up in brown paper and tied with a piece of string. Tilly picked at the knots, wishing Great-Gran hadn't done it up so tight. At last she managed to undo the string, and she wound it slowly around her fingers and put it away in her coat pocket, spinning out the moment before she opened the parcel.

Inside the brown-paper wrapping was a little cardboard box, with a lid. And inside that, there was tissue paper, old and faded and fragile. Tilly lifted it up, fascinated.

Lying on a bed of more tissue paper was a glittering Christmas tree decoration

 – a tiny gold glass basket, full of crimson roses. It was so pretty – and even older than that tissue

paper, Tilly guessed. Some of the gold had rubbed off but it still shone. Lying next to it was a photograph, in black and white, and a little folded note.

Tilly opened up the note and read it eagerly.

Dearest Tilly,

Your grandma and I can't wait to see you. You are such a brave, clever girl coming all this way by yourself. Enclosed is a special little thing for you to keep. I will tell you the story tonight!

With love from Great-Gran

Tilly picked up the photo and stared curiously at the faces looking back at her. It had to be Great-Gran and her two brothers, she guessed. Alfie, Eddie and Tilly – Great-Gran's name was the same as hers. Tilly had been named after her. They were both actually named Matilda but no one ever called Tilly that. Alfie and Eddie were sitting on a wooden gate – the wide sort of gate that was the entrance to a field – balanced on the top rail. Tilly was crouching down in the grass at the bottom of the gate, with her arm round a beautiful black-and-white sheepdog.

Tilly ran her finger gently over the ruff of white fur around the dog's neck and smiled to herself. She loved Great-Gran's old dog, Tarran, and this sheepdog looked so like him. She'd have to ask Great-Gran what this dog had been like and what his name was.

Tarran had been a working sheepdog at the farm belonging to one of Tilly's uncles but he was retired now. There was no space for a dog in the flat where Tilly lived, so walks with Great-Gran and Tarran were a massive treat. Tarran was definitely Great-Gran's dog, though. He followed her around the house and even though he let other people stroke him, he didn't seem to enjoy it very much. It was as if he only put up with it because he knew Great-Gran wanted him to.

Whenever she sat down, Tarran lay on top of her feet and guarded her.

Tilly shifted in her seat, feeling the train settle into a rhythm over the tracks. They were speeding out of the city now, passing just a few houses here and there. Winter trees spread dark bare branches against the faded sky. The faint sway of the carriage rocked her and the photograph started to slip out of her fingers. Tilly blinked and snatched it back, sitting up straighter. She couldn't go to sleep! What if she missed her stop? Mum had explained to the train guard that Grandma was meeting Tilly at Newport and he'd said he'd try to make sure she got off at the right place. But what if he was busy helping somebody else?

The thing was, she hadn't slept much the night before as she'd been so nervous and excited about her trip. She'd even dreamed the whole train journey – although it had been more like a nightmare. They were almost too late for the train and then there was nowhere to sit except on the floor, and when she got off the train she'd looked back as it growled out of the station and realized that her suitcase was still on it…

Tilly shuddered and peered round the seat to look at the little luggage bay at the end of the carriage. She could see her red suitcase. She let out her breath and closed her eyes for a moment. Then she yawned an enormous yawn that seemed to come all the way from her toes. Tilly clenched her hands into fists, digging her nails into her palms to stay awake.

"It's OK," she whispered to herself. "I've set my alarm. I can't miss it."

She scrabbled in the pocket of her backpack to double-check. Her phone had been her tenth birthday present and she loved it. She was looking forward to taking some photos of Grandma, Great-Gran and Tarran. She could even send them to Mum. Tilly and Mum had set the alarm for five minutes before the train was due to arrive at Newport. So she couldn't possibly miss her stop.

It would be all right. But even so, there was no way Tilly was going to let herself fall asleep…

CHAPTER THREE

Tilly sat up with a start, her head bumping against the window as she woke. She stared out anxiously through the glass, wondering if she'd missed her station. All she could see were fields and trees. They could be anywhere.

She rubbed her eyes. The trees didn't seem the *same*, somehow... Though they were just trees, their leaves yellowing a little at the edges with the end of summer.

But it wasn't the end of summer. It was December. When Tilly had last looked through the window, the trees had been dark and leafless. Her hands clenched in panic and she realized that she was no longer holding the photo or the little cardboard box.

"You were snoring," someone giggled, next to her ear.

"You sounded like a pig! Snorrrrrt!" Another voice joined in, with a long, loud snort, and Tilly brushed her hair out of her eyes, her strange confusion forgotten. She'd been dreaming – how long had she been asleep for? Alfie and Eddie were being naughty, and Mum had told her to make sure they behaved.

"Brothers…" Tilly muttered to herself. Then she blinked, confused. She didn't *have* a brother. Let alone two. It was just her and Mum – it always had been.

So how was she sitting in this train with two little brothers and wearing a pink cotton dress instead of leggings and her Christmas jumper? It wasn't the same train, either. Instead of one long carriage with rows of seat along either side, she was in a little room with two rows of seats facing each other, and there was a corridor running down the side of the carriage, which must lead to more little rooms.

Compartments, that's what they were called. This train was ancient – it was a steam train, too, she could smell the smoke and Alfie had coal smuts on his face.

Tilly shook herself, trying to clear away the strange fuzziness in her head. It was as if – as if she had two lives at once. But the one where she was off on her own to Grandma's, with her backpack and her mobile and her bright red suitcase, seemed thin and odd and hardly real…

The littlest boy was bouncing up and down on the seat, still snorting. Tilly blinked the odd dream away.

"Shh! Stop it, Eddie. There's other people on the train, not just us. Remember

what Mum said. You'll get in trouble."
She put her finger to her lips and scowled
at him, trying to look stern, the same
way Mum did.

Eddie just smirked at her and snorted
again but this time Tilly ignored him.
"How long was I asleep for?" she asked
Alfie. "I feel all dopey."

"You're dopey all the time," Alfie
sniggered and dodged away as she went
to poke him in the side. "Oi!"

"Are you all right, you three?"
Miss Jennings was walking along the
corridor and she put her head round the
compartment door, smiling at them.

"Yes, Miss. Thank you, Miss,"
Tilly said at once. She didn't want the
teacher to think her little brothers were
a nuisance.

"I should think we'll be there soon,"
Miss Jennings told her. "Be good, boys."

"See? Even Miss Jennings could see you
were messing about!" Tilly said crossly to
Eddie as she watched the teacher carry on
past. "And I was *not* snoring. You don't

even know what a pig sounds like. You've never seen one."

"Nor have you!" Alfie pointed out. "You reckon there'll be animals where we're going, Tilly?"

Tilly shrugged. "Suppose so. It's the country, isn't it?" As far as she knew, the country was full of animals. "Mum said maybe sheep," she added doubtfully.

"We saw sheep!" Eddie said excitedly. "We saw them while you were asleep. But they weren't all white and fluffy. They were skinny. Why were they skinny?"

"I don't know." Tilly shook her head. "We'll get to know all that sort of thing. You can ask someone," she added vaguely.

"I'm bored," Eddie wailed. "I want my bunny." He clambered down and started to look for his toy rabbit.

Tilly looked at him worriedly. They'd been on this train for ages – she wasn't sure quite how long exactly as she'd lost her sense of the time, being asleep. She should have asked her teacher how much longer.

"We'll be there soon, Miss Jennings said we would. Here's your bunny, Eddie, look." She grabbed the greyish lump from where it had fallen under the seat. It had been a bunny once but Eddie had sucked its ears to strings and it always looked grubby, however often Mum washed it. "Come and sit here with me." Tilly patted the seat beside her.

Eddie pressed the bunny against his cheek but he still didn't look happy. Luckily Alfie pointed out of the window just in time to distract his little brother. "Look! Those sheep again!"

"Oh…" Tilly looked at them, frowning a little. "You're right. They aren't fluffy at all." The sheep were grazing on the side of a hill, not far from the railway line. "Look how high up they are!" she exclaimed, trying to peer back behind them as the train rattled on. "Did you see? All up on those steep bits. With rocks everywhere."

Alfie nodded. "Looked like they might fall off."

"I thought sheep lived in fields," Tilly murmured, half to herself. It felt as if she had a lot to learn about the countryside. It was a scary feeling – but at the same time, just a little bit exciting to be going somewhere new.

Eddie kneeled up on the seat and lunged over Tilly to press his pudgy little hands against the window. His fingers left smudgy marks, Tilly noticed, feeling guilty. Mum would have made him wipe his hands after he'd eaten the bread and cheese she'd wrapped up for them. But they hadn't a cloth or any spare water. How was she supposed to get him clean? Both her brothers looked a bit grubby already, and Mum had said to look tidy and smile nicely when they arrived and then a lovely family would take them in. Tilly wasn't sure a lovely family would want them just now...

"Where are the houses?" Eddie asked, looking back at her, confused. "It's all grass. And trees. Tilly, where are the houses?"

Eddie was right. Tilly didn't think she had actually seen a house, not since she'd woken up. The landscape was empty, apart from those scattered sheep. "There!" she gasped, patting Eddie's hand and pointing. "See? A little house. Over there."

It was far in the distance, halfway up the side of another hill. A small, low place, built of grey stone. It looked as though perhaps it had been built from the same rocks that were scattered all the way down the hillside. It clung to the steep slope determinedly, huddled there against the wind.

"Is that all?" Eddie asked, his voice very small. "Are we going to live there?"

"I don't know where we're going to live," Tilly said, wrapping her arms round him. "A village, Mum said. And they said that at school, too, didn't they? Quiet and safe, out in the country. Mum thought it might be somewhere in Wales... It'll be good."

"What if it isn't?" Alfie said huskily. "What if they're mean?"

"They won't be!" Tilly swallowed hard. She had been thinking the same thing, ever since they'd been told that they had to be evacuated.

Tilly peered up at the coat and hat, now folded up in the rack above their heads with their pillowcase bundles.

Would it really be winter weather before they went back home?

CHAPTER FOUR

Eddie was snivelling and he wouldn't stop. Tilly couldn't blame all the people who looked at them and then hurried on by. They were probably the least nice-looking of all the children there.

Alfie on his own would have been snapped up at once, she thought. Lots of the women who passed through the church hall had stopped to look at him. Even though he was slumped wearily on his chair, he was still quite neat. He had a decent coat and good shoes that one of their cousins had passed down before he wore them out. Tilly's hair was all tangled and she was sure her face was dirty, and Eddie had cried trails of snot all down the front of her good pink dress. It was all over him, too, however hard Tilly had tried to wipe him with her handkerchief.

Tilly had tried to ask if they could go and have a wash, tidy themselves up a bit. But Miss Jennings looked exhausted, too – her hair was sticking out of its neat bun. She'd just smiled at Tilly and cut her off, turning away with a murmured, "Don't worry, dear," as she hurried away to see about something more important.

Tilly shifted Eddie a little. He was falling asleep against her shoulder and she was getting pins and needles. Mum had told her to make sure they were looking their best. She had tried so hard to give them everything that was on the list that the school had sent, so that no one would think they weren't nicely cared for. Most of the month's housekeeping money was gone already, Tilly reckoned, and it was only the first of September. Now it had all been wasted.

"I'll take this one."

Tilly looked up sharply. A woman about her mother's age was standing in front of Alfie. "Come along," she said to him, holding out her hand.

Alfie blinked at her and slid off the chair, reaching up his hand obediently. From the way the woman spoke, it was clear that she expected him to do as he was told. Her voice wasn't unkind, just firm. For a moment, the voice held Tilly, too. Then she gave a little jump and shifted Eddie off her lap on to Alfie's chair so she could grab at Alfie.

"No!"

The woman holding Alfie's hand looked down at her in surprise.

"I mean, no, sorry, you can't take him. Not on his own. We have to go together, my mum said."

The woman looked at her and Eddie, sleepily grizzling and obviously about to work himself up into a full wail. "Oh. I'm afraid I can only take one child," she said kindly, stepping back.

Tilly watched her walk on down the line, looking the other children over. *It's like she's shopping*, she thought suddenly. *She's like Mum at the market, looking us all over. She'll be prodding us, in a minute, to see if we're fresh.*

"You three!" The woman who seemed to be in charge at the hall bore down on Tilly, frowning. Mrs Leigh, the other ladies helping had called her. She was here, there and everywhere, clutching a pile of notes, her smart little heels clicking over the wooden floor of the hall. "There are very few houses willing to take three children, particularly not two little ones. You really will have to be separated." She smiled at Tilly. "You won't be far away, dear. We'll make sure of that. And besides, you'll still see your brothers at school, won't you?"

Tilly shook her head determinedly. "No! You mustn't. I promised Mum! I have to look after them, she said so. We have to be together."

She set her face in a stubborn scowl and Mrs Leigh shook her head, shuffling her handfuls of papers. "I really don't know what we'll do with you," she murmured, as she hurried away to fill out a form for the woman who had wanted to take Alfie.

Tilly's scowl set harder as she looked around the room. It had been so full when they'd first arrived, trailing along the road from the station. There had been a whole carriage's worth of children from her school, if not more, and then the people from the village, lined up in groups along the wall, eyeing them all. Now more than half the children were gone, maybe even two-thirds, and the only adults were latecomers, trickling in one by one. What would happen if nobody wanted them? *Perhaps they'll send us home?* Tilly thought, with a sudden leap inside her. *We can't stay here if no one will take us, can we?*

She looked down at Eddie, whimpering himself back to sleep against her shoulder, and for a moment felt almost glad that he was clutching that grubby bunny. Except – it was probably just a silly wish. If Mrs Leigh couldn't find anyone who *wanted* three children, she would beg and bully someone who didn't. Tilly had already heard her persuading one worried-looking woman into taking two girls, when she'd only planned on one. She rubbed at her cheeks, trying to brush away the smudges from the coal dust and force some colour into them. She made herself smile a little and pulled up Eddie's wrinkled socks. But it didn't seem to make any difference. Everyone just kept on walking past. No one seemed to think that she could hear but of course she did, even though the accent was hard to understand.

"I need a good strong lad to help out, not little ones."

"Sickly looking child, that one…"

"Three! I can't take three."

"Now, Mrs Jones, don't you think you could fit them in? I'm sure you have the room…" Mrs Leigh sounded posh, like some of the teachers at school, but lots of the women she was talking to had odd, lilting voices. Tilly supposed it was because they were near to Wales.

At least, she thought they were. That was where Mum had been told they were probably going.

Tilly looked down worriedly at their pillowcase bundles, hoping that the postcard was still in hers. They had to send it back, to tell Mum where they were. She shifted Eddie so he was leaning on Alfie instead. Then she could go through the bundle and make sure. He grumbled a little but didn't wake up, and Tilly leaned down to grab her pillowcase. She started searching through it frantically, looking for the thin slip of card. What if she'd lost it? What if Mum and Dad never knew where they'd ended up?

"You two going to come along of me, then?"

Tilly straightened up quickly and

gasped. What seemed like an enormously tall man was staring down at them, with a wolf-faced black-and-white dog pressed up close against him. Tilly had never been that close to a dog, not that she could remember. No one had space for a dog in the flats where they lived – or the money for feeding one.

"Mr Thomas! Really, that dog shouldn't be in here." Mrs Leigh was hurrying over, waving her lists.

The tall man ignored her and nodded to Alfie. "You'd better wake up your little brother, son. Bring him along. I'll take both of you."

Mrs Leigh brightened up. "Both of them? Oh, good, good. Lovely children, I'm sure." She cast a glance over Eddie's dirty face and forced a smile. "No one shows to good account after a long journey, you know."

"Mmm. Come on, then." The man lifted Eddie off the chair, scooping him up and holding him on his hip, just like Mum did. He turned, as if he was about to walk out, and Alfie scrambled to follow.

"No!" Tilly didn't yell this time. She

was too tired and too desperate and she was scared of the dog. It was so close and it was staring at her with shiny, orangey-brown eyes. They were like the mint bullseyes that Alfie always begged Dad to buy, if there was a penny spare for sweets.

"Don't worry, dear." Mrs Leigh put a hand on her shoulder, pushing Tilly back down on her chair. "You'll see them tomorrow." Tilly opened her mouth to argue but nothing came out.

"Mister! Hey, Mister." Alfie pulled at the tail of the man's jacket. "We have to go together. You haven't got Tilly."

The tall man turned back, looking Tilly up and down. His eyes were dark and narrow, and Tilly shrank back against her chair.

"She's with you? Your sister?" He shook

his head. "I can't take a girl. There's only me at the farm. I…" He hesitated. "I can't take care of a girl. Can someone else take her?" he asked Mrs Leigh.

"Yes, yes, of course." She ushered him on. "No one's asking you to take all three of them, Mr Thomas. We just need to fill in the forms. Over to the table here."

"No…" Tilly whispered. "I promised…" But they were already halfway across the room. Halfway to the door.

The dog wasn't, though. It was still standing in front of her, staring.

"Go on," Tilly whispered faintly. "Get away."

The man noticed at last that the dog wasn't with him. He turned back, looking surprised. Tilly supposed he was used to having it by his side always. It had been squashed up next to him, the way Alfie always was if they went anywhere with Dad. Like he was sewn on to Dad's trouser leg.

"Tarran!" he said, not even shouting. As if he didn't need to shout, as if he could have whispered and he still knew the dog would come.

Except that it didn't. It looked round at him but it didn't move. It eyed him for a moment and then turned its head to face Tilly again.

The man frowned, his heavy black eyebrows drawing together, deepening the heavy creases above his nose.

"Tarran!" His voice was a little louder this time and now the dog seemed worried, too. It swung its tail from side to side and whined, very quietly.

Eddie was awake now, peering up at the man, and Alfie was staring, too. He looked hopeful. "Is Tarran the dog's name, Mister?"

"Yes." The man strode back to the line of chairs, with Alfie and Mrs Leigh trailing behind him. He glared down at Tilly and then at the dog. "What have you done to him, then?" he muttered.

"I didn't… I never…" Tilly stammered. She didn't want the dog looking at her like that! "I didn't touch him, I swear."

The man scowled again. "Get your things."

Tilly looked up at him for a moment, her mouth half-open. She then reached down for her bundle.

"That all of it?"

She nodded at him.

"All right." He turned to Mrs Leigh. "Her as well, then. Let's get these forms done."

Tilly looked anxiously at the dog, wondering if it would bite her if she moved. She didn't know about dogs, except that Mum said they were dirty and they bit. She could see this one's teeth and its long pink tongue was hanging out. Its breaths were loud and huffing, and she wasn't sure if that meant it was angry. But then it stepped forwards and pushed at her, hard, nudging her with its muzzle.

Tilly hunched away from it and it nudged her again, harder, shoving her off the chair. It nosed her across the floor after Alfie and Eddie, its ears laid flat, until she was standing behind the man. Then it scurried round to press itself up against the man's leg again, looking pleased with itself. Tilly didn't know how she could tell but she could. It was the way its ears pricked up and the way it glanced round to check that she was still where it had put her. It was definitely pleased. *Job well done*, those ears said, Tilly was sure.

CHAPTER
FIVE

"It's too quiet," Alfie whispered. "And dark. I want to sleep with you. Please, Tilly?" He turned to look behind him at the darkness of the passageway and then fixed her with wide, fearful eyes.

Tilly pushed herself up on her elbows. There was plenty of room in her bed. It was meant for one person, she thought, but it wasn't much smaller than the bed the three of them slept in together at home. She had never expected to be given a room to herself but Mr Thomas had led them upstairs after a supper of bread and cheese, and shown her in here and the two boys next door. Tilly had unpacked her pillowcase bundle into a chest of drawers, the whole thing to herself. She'd only filled up one of the drawers, the others were rattlingly empty. She had found a red hair ribbon, though, in one of them, tucked in the join between the side of the drawer and the base. She had looked at it and put it back.

"We can't leave Eddie on his own. What if he wakes up?" she pointed out to Alfie. "He'd have kittens."

"S'pose," Alfie muttered. "It's *dark*. Don't like it."

"I don't, either. But it's this blackout. Mister said he'd get the proper curtains, or blinds or something, and then we can have candles. And it's not that dark, not really." The evening was still half light – she could see Alfie quite easily, hunched up against the doorframe. He was wearing pyjamas, blue striped ones that Mum had bought. He'd never had them before, they'd always just slept in their vests and pants. Tilly had a nightdress, a white one, like little girls in pictures.

She looked around the little room, admiring the faded flowered paper on the walls and the wood-framed mirror standing on top of the chest of drawers, with a china jug and washing bowl. She heaved a regretful sigh and swung her feet out of bed on to the rag rug. She hauled up the cover off the bed and wrapped it round her shoulders. "You can't sleep in here and leave Eddie. I'll come and sleep down the end of your bed."

Alfie nodded eagerly and hurried back along the passage to his own door, looking back to make sure she was following. Tilly shuffled along after him, the cover shushing over the chilly wooden boards. She felt like a queen, wrapped in a royal cloak. She had never seen a bedcover like this one before, pieced together out of little scraps of fabric, striped and flowery and silky-soft. She had been lying there, learning the feel of each piece under her fingers, when Alfie had come creeping in.

Tilly huddled up on the end of Alfie's bed, feeling his feet pressed against her. Eddie was fast asleep on the other side of the room, a huddled hump under his blanket, breathing in soft little wheezes.

"Got to send that postcard," Tilly whispered to herself as she fell asleep. "Mum and Dad don't even know where we are." That was the worst thought and she sniffed back tears.

"*Don't*, Eddie. Ugh. Don't lick me." Tilly woke up, swiping at her cheek. Brothers were disgusting. She blinked, expecting to see Eddie leaning over and smirking at her. That low chuckle certainly wasn't one of her brothers, though.

Tilly woke up properly and saw that

the dog was staring at her, its pink tongue hanging out as it made that huffing noise again. It almost looked as if it were *smiling*. She wriggled back, pressing herself against the wall but the dog followed her and licked her cheek again. She could see its teeth.

Mr Thomas was standing behind the dog. Had she heard him laugh, when she told Eddie to stop? He looked grim-faced now.

"I – I…" She looked around, realizing that she was in the wrong bedroom. "We always sleep together at home," she whispered. "Alfie was lonely." She wriggled her cold feet – Eddie had climbed into bed with her and Alfie sometime during the night and stolen the bottom half of the quilt. He was staring up at Mr Thomas from under the edge.

"Breakfast's ready," was all he said, before he stomped out of the room, the dog following like a shadow.

Tilly uncurled herself from the quilt and shook Alfie. He'd slept through the whole conversation.

"Breakfast!" she hissed. "Now! Come on!"

They hurried downstairs to find Mr Thomas sitting at the kitchen table, with an enormous teapot and a pan full of greyish-white stuff.

"I want bread and jam," Eddie whispered, clutching at Tilly's skirt.

"It's porridge." They stared at him and Mr Thomas looked almost worried for a moment. "Haven't you ever had porridge?"

Tilly shook her head.

He sighed and got up to open a cupboard, bringing out a tin. "Better have syrup on it, then. Don't you go getting used to it, mind. Rationing's going to start, so they say on the wireless." He lifted Eddie on to a chair and dolloped porridge into a bowl in front of him, then levered open the green tin with the end of Eddie's spoon. He drizzled a golden spiral of syrup on to the porridge and then handed the spoon to Eddie. "Get it while you can, half-pint."

Alfie swiftly sat down at the table, eyeing the syrup tin and Tilly followed him. As she sat down, a solid weight landed on her knees and she gave a tiny gasp. She peered down under the table, and saw that the dog had settled its muzzle on her lap and was gazing up at her.

Mr Thomas saw where she was looking and snorted. "He must reckon you're the softest touch, girl. He thinks you'll feed him," he added, when she stared at him blankly.

"He likes you," Alfie pointed out to Tilly and she realized that he sounded jealous.

"Does he?" she asked Mr Thomas, surprised.

"Reckon so. He made me take you, didn't he?"

Tilly nodded and started to eat her porridge. It didn't taste of a lot, the bits that weren't syrupy, but it was all right. Tarran *had* made Mr Thomas take her, she thought slowly, as she ate. She ought to be grateful. He wouldn't have done it, not without the dog. She ate slowly, leaving gaps between the spoonfuls of porridge so that when the farmer was pouring himself another mug of tea, she could whip the last spoonful under the table. Tarran licked at it so eagerly he scrubbed her fingers with his tongue, too. It tickled. Tilly pressed her lips together, trying not to laugh.

Miss Jennings looked around the clean, sunny kitchen, her face relieved. "This looks nice, Tilly," she said, smiling. "Aren't you lucky that Mr Thomas was able to take all three of you? Mrs Leigh's spent all morning driving me around, trying to find everyone."

"Yes, Miss." Tilly nodded hard. "We're very lucky. The boys like it here – Mister showed us the animals and all."

"They're a long way out of the village, for school," Mr Thomas said. He had his arms folded and he was looking at Miss Jennings and Mrs Leigh as if he was expecting them to complain about something.

Miss Jennings only sighed. "So are most of the children, to be honest. I think we'll be doing well just to get everyone there. And even if we do, there isn't the room for us. We've doubled the size of the school in a day. That's what I came to tell you, we're taking turns to share the building – it'll be school in the afternoons for you three, for now at least. Starting tomorrow, from two o'clock. Perhaps you can do some jobs around the farm in the mornings? Or help to keep house?"

Alfie looked delighted. If Miss Jennings said they had to help… He and Eddie and Tilly had been following Mr Thomas and the two farmhands around the little yard all morning. "Can I feed the pig, Mister?" he burst out hopefully. "We've got to help – she says!" He had spent at least half an hour hanging over the side of the pig's pen, scratching her back with a stick the way Mr Thomas had shown him and murmuring to her. Tilly couldn't see why – the smell had been worse than the lavatories back home on a hot day.

But the more they helped, the better. Jack, who was in her class, was in the back of that car outside with his little sister right now, both of them looking wretched. They'd not settled, Miss Jennings said. Tilly wasn't sure what that meant but even if Mr Thomas hardly talked, he'd taken the three of them. They weren't going to give him any reason to change his mind.

"I can feed the hens," she told him, hesitating a little. She didn't like the way they skittered about and pecked round her feet, but she could put up with it.

"And the little lad can hunt for eggs," the farmer agreed, his frown fading a little. "A bit of help would be welcome," he admitted. "I've got a lot to do, with the sheep."

Mrs Leigh nodded and scribbled something in her notebook, looking around the kitchen. Tilly could see her disapproving of the dog, stretched out on a rag rug by the range. Probably she thought dogs should live outside. Until breakfast-time, Tilly would have agreed with her.

"It's clean," Mr Thomas told her, eyeing the notebook. "Ivy Evans comes out from the village and helps. She does the laundry and the floors."

"Oh, no one's saying that it isn't, Mr Thomas." Mrs Leigh's smile showed too many teeth, Tilly thought. "I have to keep notes, as the billeting officer, that's all. It all looks most satisfactory."

"I don't like her," Eddie whispered as they watched the car bump away down the long lane.

"Shh!" Tilly hissed, but Mr Thomas made an odd sort of coughing noise and patted Eddie on the shoulder.

"Me neither, half-pint."

Mr Thomas sat down in the armchair next to the range and eyed the three children thoughtfully. "S'pose you ought to have gone to bed," he said, looking between them and the clock. It was past eight. "If you've got to get to school tomorrow."

"We don't have to go until the afternoon, Miss Jennings said. And it isn't dark," Alfie pointed out. "Not yet."

"Mmmm. Better finish that milk and go on up." He sighed and felt at his pockets. "Drat it. Where'd I leave my pipe? Upstairs, I suppose."

"I'll bring it down," Tilly said swiftly, jumping up. She was still trying to think of anything she could do to help but it was difficult. The farmer seemed to have lived on his own for a long while. He had ways of doing things. She had tried to put the bread and cheese away in the larder earlier and nearly dropped the lid of the big brown jar he kept the bread in. She hadn't expected it to be so heavy…

It was all right for the boys. Eddie was the baby, fat-cheeked and sweet. Everyone loved him, at least when he was in a good mood and not covered in dirt. And Alfie had spent the day hurrying around after Mr Thomas like he was the Pied Piper, asking questions about the pig and the chickens, and if he could go out to the fields and see the sheep, and what was this for and why was Mister doing that. Anyone would like him, he was so strangely happy to be here. Only Tilly didn't quite fit – and she was the one who hadn't been wanted.

"I'll fetch it – we're going up anyway. Where is it, Mister?"

He nodded to her. "On the chest in my bedroom. Down the end of the passage from you."

Tilly shepherded the other two upstairs, carrying a jug of hot water from the range, and left them washing while she went to find the pipe. They hadn't been in this room and she peered round the door as it creaked open. Another quilt, those same little pieces sewn together – a patchwork quilt, Mr Thomas had called it, when she tried to ask him about it at breakfast. Some of the pieces were the same fabrics as hers but they were mostly darker colours. Hers had been chosen to be brighter then, she realized.

She spotted the chest and hurried over to fetch the pipe and the tobacco pouch that was next to it. But then she stopped. At the back of the chest were two framed photographs. A wedding portrait – Mr Thomas, but younger, with a pretty dark-haired woman in a long dress. Then a girl with the same dark hair, not that much older than Tilly, staring solemnly out of the frame.

There *had* been a girl living here. Tilly swallowed, thinking of her bedroom, with the pretty flowered paper and the quilt. Perhaps her mother had made it for her. But where were they both?

I can't take care of a girl, Mr Thomas had said at the hall. Not because he didn't know how – but because she would remind him too much of what he'd lost.

Tilly snatched up the pipe and pouch, and made for the stairs.

CHAPTER
SIX

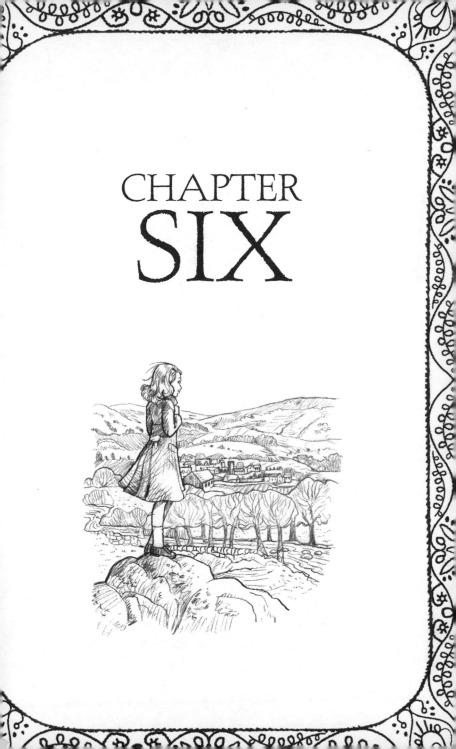

Dear Tilly,

I can't believe it's almost Christmas and you've been away for over three months. There was a Salvation Army band playing Christmas music on my way home last night and I remembered listening to them with you three this time last year. "O Come All Ye Faithful", my favourite. I missed you so much. But you sound like a proper little country girl, talking about fetching eggs and the boys feeding the pig! We're so glad that you're well and happy...

"Tilly!"

Tilly jumped and stared guiltily at Miss Jennings but the teacher was smiling at her.

"You were miles away. I need you singing up, Tilly, you've got a lovely voice."

Tilly nodded. "Sorry, Miss…" She slipped her hand into the pocket of her cardigan, feeling her mum's letter crinkle against her fingers.

Over three months. When they'd first arrived, Tilly had been counting the days, wondering when they'd be able to go home. Some of the others had gone already. Jack Brown and his little sister had never settled, and their dad had come to fetch them home. No bombs had fallen on Birmingham, Mr Brown had told Miss Jennings. Why shouldn't they come back?

But Dad had written to Tilly and the boys, saying they should stay. Things might be worse before they were better, he'd said. He and Mum wanted to be sure that they were safe.

Tilly stared at the blackboard but the carol words had gone blurry. It didn't really matter. She knew "O Come All Ye Faithful" anyway – it was her favourite, too.

Miss Jennings clapped excitedly as they finished. "That was beautiful. Just think how good you'll be by the time we give the carol concert. The morning children are practising the same carols, so that we can all sing together. But you must learn the words," she added. "We can't have anyone mouthing along. You've all copied them down into your books. Those of you with younger brothers and sisters, please help them learn their parts, too."

Tilly rolled her eyes at Mary Lewis, who'd lived in the next street back home and had a little brother as well. How exactly were they supposed to do that? Alfie and Eddie spent every spare moment outside, and Mary had said Jim was the same. Even now that it was December and icy cold, there was so much space to run, so much to look at and explore.

Yesterday morning, Tilly had climbed all the way to the top of one of the hills behind the farmhouse. She'd stood there on the mossy rock, higher than anything else, and had felt as tall as the sky. She could see for miles, and all the houses looked like toys. School felt more of a hardship here than it ever had back home.

She could see Alfie fidgeting in the front

row this minute, stretching his neck to look out of the window. This morning the frost flowers on her bedroom window had been on the inside of the glass and the puddles out in the yard had been transformed to a sheet of ice. Alfie and Eddie had fought a duel with icicles as long as rulers that dripped from the guttering. The stream was frozen over, one of the other boys had told them as they hurried into the classroom that afternoon. Tilly had promised that they'd go and look, on the way home. Just for a little while though. It would be dark by the time they got back otherwise, she reminded Alfie. He'd sniffed as if he didn't care but she knew he didn't like going up the lane either, with the light draining out of the sky and all the shadows gathering.

"We'd better be clearing up," Miss

Jennings murmured, looking over at the younger ones, who were making paper chains at the back of the classroom out of old newspapers and flour and water paste. Tilly remembered doing the same herself at their old school last Christmas but they'd had bright coloured paper to use and proper glue. Now it seemed that even coloured paper was too precious to cut up and had to be hoarded, in case. Tilly wasn't sure in case of what.

Still, Eddie and the others had created a great mass of paper chains, spilling off the desk in a jumbled heap. "Look!" He held his up to show Tilly, the newspaper coloured in with great swirls of crayon, and then wrapped it around his neck like a scarf. "I'm taking it home," he whispered. "I want to show it to Mister. And Tarran."

"All right." Tilly nodded. "You'll have to wear it, though, I've got the books to carry."

"The stream, Tilly!" Alfie had his coat on already and he tugged eagerly at Tilly's sleeve. "Hurry up!"

"I know – I know. Just let me get my coat." Tilly followed him out into the cloakroom, pulling on her coat with one hand while she wound Eddie up in gummy paper chains under his scarf.

The wind was bitter as they came out of the school porch, sending Eddie staggering sideways. Tilly grabbed his hand and Miss Jennings watched them a little worriedly as they set off. "At least it's blowing in the right direction, Tilly," she called. "It'll blow you home!"

Tilly waved to her teacher and they half ran down the street, bowled along by the wind and following the clutch of other children, all making for the stream that ran along one side of the village church. Tilly and Alfie and Eddie had searched for fish in it during those hot September days after they'd first arrived, and one of the girls from the village had shown them a water vole's hole. Now the little stream was still, the ice dark and brownish green under the trees.

"You can see the weeds frozen in it," Tilly murmured, crouching on the bank to look. "Don't you dare," she added, as Alfie went to climb down on to the ice. "It'll give way!"

"It won't, it's solid. Look, *he's* walking

on it." Alfie pointed to one of the older boys, who was sliding on the ice further up the stream. He was just about to step on to the ice, when an unnatural silence fell on the children gathered on the bank. Tilly looked round to see Mrs Leigh marching across from the vicarage, waving.

"What does *she* want?" someone muttered. As the billeting officer, it was Mrs Leigh's job to check on all the evacuees and their host families, and it wasn't only Mr Thomas who didn't like her much. She had her nose in everywhere, he said, and most of the children agreed.

"Hurry along home, all of you," she said now. "It's going to snow, can't you see? Look at that sky!"

Tilly looked up, frowning. As far as she could see, the sky was just grey – perhaps an odd, yellowish sort of grey but that was all. Did that mean snow? It had to be cold enough, Tilly thought.

Mrs Leigh stood there watching, her coat huddled over her shoulders. "Off you go."

The boy on the ice reluctantly let the

others haul him up to the bank again, and grumbling and sighing, they set off home.

"I wish we lived closer to the village," Alfie said, shoving his hands in his pockets. "I bet the others nip back out, as soon as that old witch has gone."

Tilly pushed another log into the range and then crouched in front of it, toasting her hands. Alfie and Eddie had disappeared when they reached the farm to find Mr Thomas out in the sheep fields and say hello to Sam and Davey, the farmhands.

There was a scuffle outside the back door and Tilly got up to open it. Tarran looked up at her gratefully and made for the range. He was a skinny dog and even with his thick fur Tilly was sure he felt the cold. Tilly could hear her brothers chattering as they ran across the yard. "Tilly! Mister says it *is* going to snow! Mrs Leigh was right!"

Tilly shivered by the door as they kicked off their boots. Mr Thomas had found them all wellingtons from somewhere. They were too big but Tilly's plimsolls had lasted no more than a week or so in the dusty lanes, and Alfie and Eddie had both grown out of their shoes. When Tilly had asked – worrying that Mum and Dad wouldn't be able to pay for them – he had winked at her and said, "Beg, borrow or steal, girl." And then he'd added, more gently. "Don't worry yourself."

"Looks like it to me," Mr Thomas said, as he stopped to unlace his own boots.

"Sky's had that colour to it all afternoon. Heavy-looking."

Tilly peered out into the darkness. They had torches for the walk back from school now but the batteries were already hard to get hold of. Mr Thomas took a kerosene lamp when he went out around the yard and the fields late in the evening.

"When's it going to snow?" Alfie demanded excitedly, still gazing out into the yard as if he expected to see the flakes circling down. "Will it settle?"

"It's cold enough." Mr Thomas beat his hands against his arms and stamped his feet to warm them. "That dog's stealing all the heat again, I see." But he padded over to run Tarran's silky ears through his fingers, so that the dog closed his eyes and pointed his nose to the ceiling in happiness.

Tilly thought back to last winter, the
slushy muddiness in the streets and the
aching cold of their little flat, where
there were never enough shillings for
the meter. She hoped it didn't snow back
home – Mum would freeze. Still, she had
a shift now at the same factory as Dad –

it was probably warm there, with all the machines going.

"It is!" Alfie suddenly squealed. He turned back from the door, pointing frantically. "Look! Look, it is!"

"Are you making it up?" Tilly was too used to Alfie teasing her. She would look and then he would collapse into giggles. But his eyes were so wide... She peered over his shoulder and caught her breath. It was hard to see, with the oil lamps burning in the kitchen – only a faint golden wash of light spilled out into the yard – but he was right. Slow, heavy flakes were falling, sugar-white.

"The poor sheep," Tilly murmured, watching as the snow grew thicker. "Shouldn't they be inside?"

"In here?" Mr Thomas grinned at her.

"You want them in bed with you, girl?"

"No…" Tilly held up her hands, trying to explain. "Don't they have a shed?"

"They stay out all year round – they give birth out on the hills, even. We bring them in for shearing, that's all." He patted her shoulder. "They gather together and shelter each other. And their fleece is waterproof – better than your coat, girl. They're only in danger if they're caught in a drift."

A drift? Tilly shivered, and shooed Alfie and Eddie back inside. Then she pushed the door shut against the snow. "We're letting out light," she told them, her voice sharp. "We aren't supposed to do that. Blackout, remember."

CHAPTER
SEVEN

"Get up! Get up! Look!"

Tilly groaned, pulling the quilt and the two extra blankets back over her head, but Eddie was bouncing on top of her. "It snowed! It snowed more! It's all everywhere!"

When they had gone to bed the night before, there had been a thin crust of white over the roofs and the yard. Now the yard was covered in a thick layer of snow, sparkling in the morning light. Out in the yard, Mr Thomas was digging a pathway towards the gate and the fields.

"Let's go and help!" Alfie sprang off Tilly's bed and dashed back next door to get dressed, with Eddie racing after him. A minute or so later she heard them clattering down the stairs and falling over each other to put on their wellingtons.

Then they spilled out into the snow, without even coats. Tilly edged slowly out of her quilt, wincing as the cold hit her, and hurried to dress.

All she'd meant to do was get Eddie and Alfie back inside before they froze or soaked their clothes, but as she stepped out into the yard, the silence wrapped itself around her. The boys had raced off down the lane to see how deep the snow was – she could hear them shrieking and giggling in the distance. Here in the yard, the snow had softened and hushed everything. As Tilly stepped out, it crunched under her boots and she laughed in surprise. It was so clean, it glittered. She had seen snow before, of course, but never without a gang of other children racing all around her, flinging snowballs. She had never realized how quiet it was – or how bright. She crouched down, tucking up the hem of her woollen skirt so that it didn't trail, and scooped up a handful of snow. She could feel it melting into her mitten almost at once but she didn't care. The snow wasn't white, she realized, examining the little mound. It was clear – hundreds and thousands of tiny ice crystals piled together.

"Tilly! Tilly! There's snow everywhere!" The boys came skidding and pounding back. "Mister says there's a sledge in the outhouse. Come on, we're going to find it." They darted past her, stomping channels across the clean snow.

Tilly sighed for the lost whiteness of it – but then, a sledge! She had never been on a sledge. She sprang up and dashed after them.

The shadowy outhouse was full of things that had been shoved away and forgotten. Alfie and Eddie were too busy trying to work their way around the piles of old machinery and boxes of junk to look but Tilly caught her breath at the sight of a battered crib, half-covered in ancient-looking curtains. Surely the sledge must have belonged to Mr Thomas's daughter, too? But he had told the boys it was there – he didn't mind them using it.

"I can see it!" Alfie yelped. "Up there, look, hanging on the wall. Tilly, can you reach it?"

Tilly nodded, stepping carefully around the old crib and lifting the wooden sledge off the hooks. It was heavier than she had expected, solid wood with metal-capped runners and a worn rope handle.

"Look at it," Alfie whispered admiringly, as Tilly staggered back. "Here, careful, Tilly, you'll drop it!"

"It's heavy! Ooof. There." Tilly laid it down in the doorway and Alfie grabbed the handle, pulling the sledge gently across the snow.

Eddie tumbled out after them, jumping up and down. "Can I have a go? Can I go on it? Please?"

"All right." Alfie nodded. "I'll pull you. But then we have to take turns."

Eddie climbed on to the sledge, giggling to himself, his cheeks scarlet with excitement and cold. Alfie ran forwards, hauling on the rope. The sledge skidded smoothly across the snow on its metal runners and Eddie shrieked, "Faster! Faster!"

"Ah, you found it." Tarran came sniffing curiously around the sledge and Mr Thomas stomped through the snow to crouch down beside them. "Looks all right. Rope isn't rotten, then? You don't want that giving way halfway down a hill."

Alfie pulled on it experimentally and Eddie tumbled backwards, nearly falling off. But he was too excited to care.

"Where are we going to race it?" Alfie asked. "We need a slope – but not all rocky…"

"Up there." Mr Thomas pointed to the low hills rising behind the farm. "There's a smooth run down Pierce's Hill but mind you don't go straight into the stream at the bottom." He looked at Tilly, frowning. "I need to be out with the sheep, making sure none of them are trapped further up. Can you get yourselves some of that pie from the larder, before you go off to school?"

Tilly nodded.

"Can we take the sledge to school?" Alfie asked hopefully and Mr Thomas looked out thoughtfully at the lane.

"Might not be a bad idea," he said slowly. "It'll be a hard walk back up for the little one tonight."

"It doesn't even look the same," Tilly muttered, pulling hard against the rope.

Alfie shook his head, looking at the road. "It *is* that way, isn't it?"

"Yes... It's just the snow that makes it look different. We know it's this way." They knew the way back from the village, of course they did. They had walked it almost every day for months now. But the snow had turned it into a new landscape, smoothed and blurred. Miss Jennings had sent them all home early, knowing how many of her class had to reach outlying farms, but the sky was a heavy grey already, streaked with sunset red. Tilly was sure that more snow was going to fall that night. The reddish light made the snow look even more eerie.

Tilly dragged on the rope again, shuffling determinedly through the snow. More had come down while they were in school and the fresh snow was nearly up to the top of her boots. Miss Jennings had said that they were not to come to school tomorrow if there was another heavy fall.

"My feet hurt," Alfie moaned. "Isn't it my go on the sledge? I'm tired of pulling."

"Eddie's too little to pull…"

"It isn't fair!"

"What's that?" Eddie's voice quavered as a bobbing light came around the corner, striking a strange glow off the snow-covered trees.

Tilly gulped at the dark figure striding towards them. It was odd-shaped, waveringly thin and tall. She half-crouched, making ready to seize her littlest brother from the sledge and run – where?

Then part of the strange shadow came darting out towards them and Tarran circled the children anxiously, as if they were sheep he was bringing back to their pen. He nosed at Tilly's mittened hands and she stroked him gratefully, her heart thumping with relief.

"Mister?" Alfie yelled delightedly. "You came to get us!"

Tilly let out her breath in a relieved sigh – Alfie was right. It was only Mr Thomas, with a couple of sacks tied around his neck like a strange sort of cloak to keep off the snow.

"Reckon it's going to start coming down heavy, any time now," he said, packing

Alfie on to the sledge behind Eddie. "Can you manage walking, Tilly girl?" he asked her, looking up at the sky worriedly.

Tilly nodded. "Course."

It was the first time he had called her by her name.

CHAPTER
EIGHT

Dear Tilly,

I'm glad to hear that you are being a good girl and helping out your poor Mr Thomas. I don't know how he manages all alone with the three of you! Give my love to Alfie and Eddie. I hope to come and visit you soon but the shifts at the factory make it difficult. Is it snowing in Linchurch? There have been a few flurries here but I've heard the weather is very cold near you...

Tilly laughed, holding out the letter to show Alfie. It had been delayed by the snow. They had been completely cut off for a couple of days and when Mr Marsh the postman finally made it through that morning, he had been laden down with letters and parcels. The parcels were in a pile on the kitchen table now, and Alfie and Eddie were prodding them sneakily. Mr Marsh had told Tilly that he didn't think anything would be able to make it up their lane – he had left his van in the road and walked up to the farm.

There was a muffled sort of knocking on the kitchen door and Tilly ran to open it, wondering if Mr Marsh had found another letter for them in his bag. Instead, as she opened the door, a dark mass of branches sprang into the room.

"A Christmas tree!" Tilly breathed in its spicy scent. She had seen them in shop windows but they had never had one at home. There wasn't room. Last Christmas Dad had bought a sprig of mistletoe to hang up but a tree was magical.

"Is that for here?" Alfie asked and Eddie just stared.

Mr Thomas looked almost embarrassed. "It's not that big," he murmured. "Thought you'd like it. Only four more days until Christmas now. You've got to have something to put all those presents under, after all."

"We can put the decorations we made at school on it. Thank you," she added shyly. She put her hand on Mr Thomas's cold red one and squeezed it hard. She might have hugged him but she still wasn't sure if he would want her to. Instead she made a fuss of Tarran, who was sniffing suspiciously at the tree, obviously unsure why this bit of outside was coming in. "Do you like it?" she whispered to him, as she scratched the thick fur at his neck. "No eating the presents."

"We can put it over here," Mr Thomas said, lifting up the tree again and carrying it slowly over to the corner of the kitchen, next to the dresser. He stood it upright, steadying it in its bucket of soil, and smiled as Eddie came thundering down the stairs with his arms full of paper chains.

There would be no more school until well after Christmas, Miss Jennings had said. January sometime – who knew when the thaw would come. It should have been exciting but Tilly missed the chance to talk to the other girls, even if it had meant the long cold walk to and from the village. They had been much envied for the sledge, that first day of the snow, but some of the others had mentioned tea trays or even burlap sacks. It sounded like almost everyone had something they could slide on and there was a good steep slope at the back of the churchyard. If only the farm was a little closer in. Tilly had been looking forward to the carol concert, too – all that practising had gone to waste. Miss Jennings had said they'd do a spring show for everyone who'd missed the carols but it wasn't the same.

Still, the loneliness was forgotten in draping the tree with paper chains and mending the ones that had come unstuck with flour and water paste.

"It looks grand," Alfie said at last, leaning over from a chair to wrap the last chain round the top branches. "Where's Mister? He ought to see."

"I'll go and find him." Tilly looked out into the yard but there was no light moving around any of the sheds. She went to the bottom of the stairs, wondering if Mr Thomas had gone upstairs, but then she heard a noise in the parlour, the room off the hall that they hardly ever used. Mr Thomas went in there to listen to the news on the wireless and Tilly had sat with him sometimes to listen, too, but it wasn't a room to linger in. The chairs were stiff and the room was so little used that it smelled dusty and stuffy, even though Ivy Evans cleaned it out every week.

It was a strange sort of noise – like breathing but with a hiccup in it. Tilly felt her face redden. Crying! Torn, she stood outside the half-open door, balanced on her tiptoes, ready to turn and hurry back into the kitchen. The hitching breath came again and Tilly could almost see

Mr Thomas, pressing his sleeve against his mouth, his shoulders heaving. She pushed the door a little and stepped round it, staring at the bright patterned rug on the floor so she didn't have to look at him. So he didn't have to be seen.

"We've finished putting up the paper chains. Do you want to come and look?"

"Mmm." He gasped out a breath. "Found these for you to put on the tree, too." He thrust a small cardboard box at her and Tilly took it, looking up in surprise. It was too late to pretend she hadn't seen the shiny trails down the sides of his nose. She stared at him, too embarrassed to speak.

"They were Lucy's," he muttered, still keeping a grip on the box.

"L-Lucy's?" she stammered.

"My girl. She was younger than you, when she died. Nine. It was measles."

"Oh…" Tilly nodded. A girl in her class at school had died of measles. She and the boys had never had it. "Did your wife have measles, too?" she whispered.

"What?" He looked up. "No! No … of course, you wouldn't know. She died having Lucy. Well, two days after. Some sort of birthing sickness, the doctor said. I brought up Lucy on my own. With a lot of help from her grandmother." He sighed and carefully lifted the lid of the greyish cardboard box. It was divided into compartments, lined with tissue, and in each little square glittered a glass ornament. Most of them were coloured baubles, pink and green and gold, but there was a row of little shapes as well.

"A flower basket," Tilly whispered, stroking it with one fingertip. "It's so pretty." She ran her thumb over the shining golden basket of scarlet roses, frowning to herself. It seemed oddly familiar. As though she had seen it before but at the same time, she knew she hadn't. It was a faint, misty memory, almost like a dream.

Tilly lifted the corner of the tissue in the last square, which seemed to be empty, wondering if the ornament was hidden underneath.

"Ah, that one was broken," Mr Thomas said, smiling a little. "Tarran's fault. Lucy was cross with him for the whole of Christmas, until they were put away again and she forgave him. They were her present, you see. Mrs Hornby at the village shop had them in and Lucy loved them. She said she didn't want a doll, she wanted these, even though she'd only have them for a few days of the year." He smiled to himself and Tilly saw his eyes shine over again.

Tilly blinked. Tarran had broken it? But – how old was Tarran? She had thought that this all happened long ago, so long ago that it was almost forgotten. Mr Thomas looked old, his hair thin and grey. Too old to have a daughter not that much older than her. But if Tarran had known Lucy... "When did she die?" she whispered.

"Three years ago – no, four. Four years in January. I haven't taken these out since." He shook his head and looked at her, forcing his mouth into a smile. "We'll put them on the tree. But high up – it was Tarran's tail that knocked the missing one off a branch last time. Above tail height, they need to be."

Tilly swallowed, looking down at the baubles and thinking of Eddie and Alfie and paper aeroplanes and arguing and climbing on chairs. "What if they get broken?" she whispered. "Hadn't you better put them away safe?"

Mr Thomas shook his head. "No. We'll get them out." He patted her shoulder clumsily. "It'll be all right, Tilly. If we break another one – well. It's bound to happen. Too fine to keep hidden, these are. They're doing us no good packed away in that box."

Mr Thomas's socks were all darned, the heels and toes lumpy with different colours of wool, but they were big, which was what mattered. Eddie picked up his, shoving both his fists down inside it. "Do you think it'll be full?" he asked, stretching the wool out as far as he could.

"No." Tilly didn't want him to get too hopeful – but after all, Mr Thomas had given them the socks, hadn't he? He'd said they should hang them up by the parlour fireplace. He wouldn't have done that if he didn't think that there might be things in them. "Eddie, stop stretching it like that. It'll come undarned. It's supper time. Come on, leave the socks. We'll look in the morning, remember? To see if Father Christmas has been."

She persuaded the boys out of the room, though Eddie kept staring back hopefully, as if he expected the socks to bulge with presents at any moment. But the sight of the supper table distracted him. Mr Thomas had got Ivy Evans to make a Christmas cake for them when she was making her own. She had gossiped to Tilly about it when she brought it up in its tin, wondering whether they would be able to get the fruit and sugar for a cake like that next Christmas, now that rationing was supposed to be coming in.

Even though the cake was beautiful, smothered in thick white icing, with a tiny painted Father Christmas in the middle, Tilly had crept away and cried. Next Christmas? She had thought they would be back home by now but the war hardly seemed to have started properly. There had been fighting in Finland but that felt so far away. Tilly hardly knew where it was – she hadn't been able to find it in the school atlas until Miss Jennings had shown it to them. And even though there had been no bombs at all, Mum and Dad were determined that they had to stay.

"When can we eat it?" Eddie pleaded, sniffing at the cake. "I'm so hungry…"

"We can't cut into it!" Tilly told him. "We're waiting for Mister. He's only gone for a last check on the sheep. He said the snow was drifting again because the wind's got up. He wanted to make sure none of them were buried." She shivered a little. The wind was whistling in the chimney, making strange, wailing noises that set her teeth on edge. She hated to think of the sheep outside in that, let alone Mr Thomas and Tarran. She glanced up at the kitchen clock and blinked, surprised. Seven, already? They must have been admiring the socks in the parlour for longer than she had thought.

"He's been gone ages," Alfie said, going to the window to look for the lantern bobbing across the yard. Then he frowned, looking back over his shoulder at the clock. "He must have found some buried ones. Should we go and help? He's been gone two hours, Tilly."

"Is it that long?" Tilly looked back at the clock, too. She hadn't been sure… "I'll go and look for the lantern," she murmured. "You stay here and take care of Eddie."

"I want to come with you!"

"I'll only be five minutes, I'm just going to see if he's coming, that's all." She flung on her coat, and stuffed her feet into her thick socks and wellingtons. "Don't let him pick at that icing!"

Eddie snatched his hand back guiltily and Tilly made a face at him. Then she opened the door, her teeth clenching in a grimace at the rush of icy cold that hit her like a wall.

"Tilly, look!" Alfie pointed out across the yard.

"What?" Tilly's eyes were watering too much with the cold to see what he was pointing at. "Can you see him coming?" She blinked and rubbed her eyes – she couldn't see a light at all. "Oh! Tarran!"

The sheepdog was hurrying along the path that Mr Thomas and the children had dug across the yard, his ears laid flat.

"Good dog," Tilly called, slapping her knees. "Come on in, lovely boy. Where's Mister, hey?" She stood back to let Tarran shoot past her, the way he usually did, but the dog stopped halfway across the yard instead. He stood there and barked, two sharp barks. He was staring at Tilly, pawing at the ground anxiously.

"What is it?" Tilly asked. "Come on. It's cold out there…" She slapped her knees again and at last Tarran came up to the door. But he didn't come in. Instead he took the hem of Tilly's coat in his teeth and pulled.

"Hey!" Alfie reached out to push Tarran away, shocked, but Tilly stopped him.

"He's not being bad. Something's

wrong. He's come to get me." She looked worriedly at Alfie and Eddie. "I think something's wrong with Mister."

CHAPTER
NINE

Tilly dragged on her mittens, grabbed her torch and hurried after Tarran. "Stay inside!" she called to Alfie and Eddie, as she set off across the yard. "Keep the door shut. I'll be back soon, I promise."

She could see their pale, worried faces peeping round the blackout blind as she followed Tarran through the farmyard gate. Mr Thomas had gone to the pasture closest to the farmhouse, for a last look at the ewes in lamb. So he must be somewhere nearby, Tilly told herself. Tarran seemed to know exactly where he was going. He was hurrying on ahead impatiently, stopping every few paces to wait for Tilly to catch him up.

"What happened?" Tilly murmured to him, her voice shaking a little as she unlatched the gate into the field. She didn't expect Tarran to answer, of course. It was just that the night was so dark and quiet. The only sound was the squeak and crunch of her boots in the snow, and the scuffle of Tarran's paws. Talking to Tarran made her stomach feel less shaky, even though her voice seemed to be echoing out into the cold, empty air in the strangest way.

"How did Mister hurt himself?" Tilly stopped suddenly. "Tarran! What if he's really badly hurt?" She shone her torch worriedly at the dog up ahead but Tarran yapped at her. He just wanted her to hurry up.

"Oh, Tarran, where is he?"

A strange shape lumbered out of the darkness, and Tilly jumped and gasped.

Then she laughed at herself, even though she was so frightened. A sheep – she'd almost forgotten that they were there, they were so well disguised in the snow. They were all around her, she realized, moving the torch in a circle. Some of them stumbled to their feet, obviously wondering if she was bringing more food. Mr Thomas had told her that he had brought out some bags of sheep nuts, as it was hard for the sheep to dig down through the snow to get to the grass.

She trudged on a few more steps, circling the torch around, worried that she was going to fall over one of the sheep. The snow was trodden down where they had been digging for food and Tilly was sure that she could see a bootprint here and there. But no more snow had fallen today

– those prints could have been from this morning. She could only trust that Tarran would help her find Mr Thomas. Several of the sheep seemed to be lying down in the snow but they didn't look miserable. Or at least, she didn't think they did… She wasn't very good at understanding sheep yet.

Tarran came haring back, his tail swinging eagerly and grabbed her coat in his teeth again. "Have you found him?" Tilly gasped, breaking into a stumbling run through the packed snow. "Oh…"

Mr Thomas was sitting on the ground, hunched up against the cold. He looked up as Tilly came running towards him and smiled at her vaguely. He had lost his cap and there was a cut across his forehead. It had bled all down his jacket, and blood had dried and frozen in his hair. It was still seeping sluggishly out of the wound.

"Tilly…" he murmured. He didn't sound as worried as Tilly thought he should. More surprised than anything, as though he hadn't expected to see her out in the field in the dark.

"I came to find you!" Tilly told him, her voice sharp and cross. She heard the crossness herself and felt guilty, but she couldn't help it. Why was he just sitting there? Didn't he know how worried they had been? "We were waiting for ages," she scolded. "We didn't know what had happened! We have to go back to the house, come on."

"Mmmmm." Mr Thomas nodded and then winced but he didn't get up.

Tilly stared down at him anxiously.

Alfie had fallen down the stairs once,
back home. Just a few steps but he'd hit
his head on the banister at the bottom.
He'd been like this, she remembered.
Sleepy and vague. Mum had called out the
doctor in the end, she'd been so worried
about him. Concussion – that was what it

was called. If that was what Mister had, it must be worse because of the cold. People who fell asleep in the snow lay down and never got up – that was what one of the boys at school had said, when they were all talking about the snow on that first day. Miss had told him off for scaring the little ones but she had told them that it was true, cold could be very dangerous. It made people's bodies slow and sleepy, she'd explained. It felt too hard to move and they just wanted to curl up in the snow and rest...

Tilly crouched down next to Mr Thomas. "We've got to get you home," she said, trying to sound encouraging instead of angry and frightened. She wanted to scream and stamp and drag him across the field at a run but that wasn't going to work. "Can you stand up, if I pull you?"

Tarran was standing next to her and Tilly could swear that he was wearing the same worried expression that she was. He leaned in closer and took Mr Thomas's sleeve in his teeth, pulling at him the same way he had dragged Tilly.

"Hello, boy..." Mr Thomas murmured. And then, "Hello, Tilly... What are you doing out here, girl?"

"Come on," Tilly coaxed, pulling at his other arm. "Can you stand up? Come on..." At last he lumbered up on to his feet, swaying a little but staying upright, and Tilly hurried to wrap his arm round her shoulders. She was so much shorter than he was, she thought anxiously. What if he just fell over again? But once he was walking, he went blundering on, seeming to follow an invisible path back through the field to the gate. He must know his way around the farm so well, she realized, that he didn't need to be properly awake. He could probably find his way back to the farmhouse in his sleep, she thought, relief bubbling up inside her.

He was leaning hard on her, though, and she kept stumbling over tussocks of grass hidden under the snow. Tarran paced in front of them, looking back to check that they were following.

"Gate…" Mr Thomas mumbled, reaching out the hand that wasn't round Tilly's shoulders. "Where's it gone?"

"It's here," Tilly told him, trying to tuck the torch under her chin so she had a hand free to unbolt the gate. "Oh!" She'd nearly dropped it. Then she felt someone gently take the torch out of her hand and she gave a little gasping chuckle. Tarran was holding it in his teeth, gazing up at her solemnly. "You're such a good boy," she whispered to him. "Good, clever dog. You rescued him, didn't you?"

"Good dog," Mr Thomas agreed, his voice thick and slurred.

Tilly dragged the gate shut behind her, her frozen fingers slipping painfully on the bolt. She pulled Mr Thomas's arm tighter round her aching shoulders and gritted her teeth hard. It wasn't much further. Just down the lane and across the yard.

"Nearly there." Mr Thomas seemed to liven up a little as they came to the farmyard gate.

"Yes," Tilly panted. "We'll be home in a minute. You'll be better in the warm." At least, she hoped he would be. But Mum had sent a neighbour running for the doctor, when Alfie wasn't as bad as this…

"They're coming! They are, look!"

That was Eddie, she realized, smiling despite herself as she saw the light from the door. "Blackout!" she hissed to him – but there was no one going past to check, was there?

"Is he all right?" Alfie yelled. "What happened?"

"I think he fell – he must have hit his head on a stone," Tilly said breathlessly, as she helped Mr Thomas through the door and across the kitchen to his armchair by the range. It was beautifully warm in the kitchen. She could feel her fingers stinging and tingling as the heat started to thaw them out.

"All that blood…" Alfie said, his face suddenly a bit green. "He looks … awful bad, Tilly."

"I know." He did look bad, she realized.

Much worse by the light of the oil lamp than he had in the wavering beam of her torch out in the field. Tarran was crouched next to the armchair, his ears laid back and the bones of his shoulders showing. He looked as scared as Tilly was. He nudged his head against Tilly's hand, gazing up at her with fearful eyes. Tilly stroked him, her numb fingers fumbling over his fur. "I ... I suppose we ought to clean him up. Mister?" she added, crouching in front of him. "Mister?"

Mr Thomas seemed to look at her – his eyes moved – but Tilly wasn't sure it was her that he was seeing. He sighed and leaned back in the chair, and as his eyes closed, a change seemed to come over his face.

"Is he asleep?" Alfie whispered.

"I don't know. I think he needs a doctor." Tilly swallowed hard. The farmhouse wasn't on the telephone, so the only way to get a doctor was to walk to the village. Should she? She knew where the doctor's house was, they passed it on the way to the school. Would the doctor even come out on Christmas Eve? She supposed he had to. Swallowing hard, she stood up and seized a couple of clean old towels from the drawer. She folded one of them up into a pad and pressed it gently over the cut.

"Get some water in a bowl," she told Alfie. She didn't want him staring at the blood any more, he looked as if he was going to pass out, too.

"Is it supper time?" Eddie asked her hopefully and Tilly pressed her lips together so as not to snap at him. He was too little to understand. "I've got to go and get someone to look at Mister's head," she explained. "Um… You can eat a slice of cake. Alfie will cut you both some in a minute."

Alfie came back with the bowl and Tilly dipped the other towel into it, wiping away the blood from Mr Thomas's face. It looked a little better.

"Tilly, you can't walk to the village," Alfie told her worriedly. "It's all snowed up."

"Mr Marsh got through," Tilly said. "Can I take your mittens? And your scarf? Mine are wet through already."

"He's big," Alfie muttered. "You aren't. And he had his van to get as far as the lane. You shouldn't go."

"Look at Mister!" Tilly hissed. "He's not well. His head's really hurt. And it maybe needs sewing up. I have to!" She snatched his scarf from the back of the chair where it had been drying in front of the range and glared at him.

Alfie swallowed and handed her his mittens.

CHAPTER TEN

Tilly swapped the lantern over to her other hand and stuffed her free hand as deep as she could into her coat pocket. Her fingers were aching with the cold already and she wasn't even down to the fork in the lane. The lantern was heavy, much heavier than her torch, but the battery had been running down as they'd struggled back across the field. She hadn't dared take it – what if it had given up, halfway to the village? Even though the lantern was hard to carry, it cast a little pool of light all around her so that it felt as if she was walking in a bubble. The light fell warm and golden on the snow – but the warmth of it was stolen away by the freezing air.

Tilly plodded on, peering at the bushes and fences, their shapes blurred by humps and lumps of snow. She seemed to have lost all her landmarks but she kept looking for them out of habit. That old bit of sacking caught in the brambles that meant she was nearly at the fork. The patch of ivy climbing up the fence. It was all covered and it left her feeling worried, uncertain. Everything was so empty, in the white of the snow, and she felt horribly alone. Surely she should have reached the road by now? The lane was only half a mile long.

There was a scratching, scuffling noise behind her and Tilly swung the light round, her heart thumping.

"Tarran!" She crouched down, dropping the lantern into the snow, and threw her arms round the dog, loving his warmth and the damp nuzzling of his nose under her chin. Now that he was there with her, she was shaking, at last admitting to herself how afraid she had been to be alone. "You shouldn't have come," she murmured. "You should have stayed at home and watched over them… We'd better be quick, Tarran. Alfie and Eddie won't be able to look after Mister if anything … happens to him."

Tarran gazed back at her and Tilly sighed. She knew how clever he was – Mr Thomas had told them that Tarran had won prizes at sheepdog trials. His eyes were bright in the lantern light but Tilly was sure that he looked worried. Tarran had chosen to come with her, instead of staying with his master, and that could only be because he knew she needed help.

Grimly she trudged on, shoving her way along the beaten-down path in the middle of the lane. Only people had walked down here, she realized. No cars or farm carts. "It'll be easier once we get to the road," she told Tarran and the dog pressed close against her legs, hearing the fear and weariness in her voice.

As they reached the road, the snow started again. Just a few flakes at first but almost within seconds a dancing flurry of white all around them. How excited they had been, a few days before, seeing the snow start to fall! Now Tilly looked around her in horror. She could hardly see and it seemed to be getting even colder now, the aching chill drawing all the warmth out of her. She forced herself on down the road, every step a great effort, the snow clumping on her boots.

"We'll just stop for a minute," Tilly whispered at last. "If I stop and rest just for a little bit, that would be all right. Five minutes…" She blundered over towards the hedge, thinking that if she crawled under it she'd be away from those stinging flakes, battering her cheeks and freezing on to her eyelashes.

Tilly sank down in the snow, huddling her arms round her knees. She could feel the cold of the ground soaking into her but at the same time a great, lazy warmth seemed to be sweeping over her body. She felt so much better. She should have rested before! She laid her head down on her knees and closed her eyes – just for a moment.

"Don't…" she mumbled, as someone dragged at her arm. "No… Let me sleep." She pushed vaguely to make them go away and then sighed, smiling to herself as she was left in peace. The snow was so warm…

Tilly came to herself with a splutter, coughing as something horrible burned in her throat.

"Ah! There you are! Yes, it's all right, dog. She's awake, look."

Tilly blinked, confused. She was in a car, she decided. She had never been in one before. Mr Thomas had driven them back to the farm that first day, squashed up in the front of his old truck, but it hadn't looked like this, with neat padded seats and piles of rugs. She stared at the man who had fed her the brandy and was now rubbing at her hands and frowning to himself. Tarran was sitting on her feet, staring up at her with dark, anxious eyes.

"Tarran…"

"Oh, that's his name, is it? Very suitable." The man smiled at her.

Tilly gazed back, wondering what on earth the man was talking about and wincing at the pain in her fingers. They felt fat and puffy, like sausages.

"It means Storm, you know. In Welsh. Lots of Welsh names here, just across the border. You're one of the evacuees from Thomas's farm, aren't you? What are you doing out here, girl? You're lucky the dog stopped me."

"Tarran made you stop?" Tilly tried to sit up straighter and force her slow wits to work. There was something important she was supposed to be doing but her head felt as if it was full of thick, dark syrup, like the syrup Mister put on their porridge...

"He was standing in the middle of the road, barking and barking. He wouldn't move, even when I hooted. As soon as I got out to see what was the matter, he led me over to you, curled up under the hedge like some little wild creature."

"Syrup... Mister... I've got to get to the doctor!" Tilly burst out, pushing weakly at the man, who was tucking another blanket round her. She glared at him – he was smiling at her as if she was talking nonsense. "I've not gone doolally, I mean it. That's where I was going. Mr Thomas needs a doctor." Pleadingly, she added. "Are you going into the village? Could you drive me to Dr Hall's on your way? Please? I don't know how long I was asleep, I shouldn't have stopped walking. He was bleeding so much…"

The man's face sharpened. "Bleeding? What happened?"

"I think he must have hit his head on a stone – Tarran came and got me, Mister was out in the sheep field. I got him back home but he's all strange, half-asleep. Please can't you take me to the doctor?"

"I *am* the doctor." The man smiled at her. "Wrap yourself back up. I was on the way back from a confinement – delivering a baby, I mean," he added, at her blank look. "They always choose the worst time to arrive." He pulled the rugs up round Tilly again and wriggled out of the back seat. "Let's hope the car starts, she doesn't like the cold." The engine growled and groaned but then it lurched forwards, skidding a little on the packed snow. "Careful, careful," Dr Hall murmured to himself or the car, Tilly wasn't sure which.

"Good boy," she murmured to Tarran, who had climbed up next to her on the back seat. Tilly pressed her cheek against the velvet of his muzzle. "That's twice you've rescued Mister. I don't suppose you even know what you've done. You should have a medal…" Tilly's voice trailed away in weariness and Tarran burrowed under the blankets and rested his nose in her lap as they crawled steadily back towards the farm.

Tilly sat on the arm of the chair, watching as Alfie and Eddie played with the toy fire engines that Mum and Dad had sent.

Her books were upstairs, carefully lined up on the shelf above her bed, with the notebook and pencils that Mr Thomas had given her. A tiny china doll was in her pocket – Mum had said that she knew Tilly was a bit old for dolls, really, but this one was so pretty, she'd had to send her. She had little white socks and black shoes painted on, and a pink dress. *She reminded me of you, the day I sent you off on that train*, Mum had written in her card.

"Happy Christmas," Mr Thomas murmured, smiling at her. "Most exciting Christmas you've ever had, I bet." He ran his hand gently over the bandage round the side of his head.

Tilly nodded and shivered. "I don't think I like exciting."

"You look tired still," he said, eyeing

her anxiously. "Maybe you should go back to bed."

"But it's Christmas Day..." Tilly smiled at him. "I can't spend it in bed!"

Tarran looked up from the rug suspiciously, as if he thought they might be about to move. He'd taken to following them both around, in case they got lost or hurt themselves again. If they weren't in the same place, he trotted between them, looking worried.

Tilly gazed sleepily at the Christmas tree, with Lucy's glass baubles glittering on it. Mr Thomas had put a branch of candles on the dresser and the flames flickered, reflected in the shining glass. She was so sleepy, full of Christmas food. The news of Mr Thomas's accident had gone back to the village with the doctor and people had been trudging up the lane all morning. Ivy Evans had brought a plate of roast chicken and Dr Hall had brought a box of chocolates with him when he drove over to check on them.

She leaned back, resting her head half on the chair and half on Mister's shoulder, listening to the Christmas music on the wireless and watching the shimmering lights on the tree…

Tilly woke with a jolt and swiped at the alarm on her phone, silencing the squeaky music. She was leaning against a hard, cold glass window, not a soft shirtsleeve. Her head was full of snow and candlelight, and the dark, shining eyes of a beautiful dog.

It was all gone. The story seemed to be fading already – she could hardly even remember their faces.

Tilly pressed her hand across her mouth to stop herself from crying out and then she stumbled up from her seat as the train began to slow down, ready to pull into the station. She dragged her red case out of the luggage rack, fought miserably with the heavy door and stepped down on to the platform, flinching as the first snowflakes began to fall softly around her.

"Tilly! You're here at last!" said Grandma Ellen, hurrying over. "Oh, I've been so looking forward to seeing you. And now it's snowing, too. Isn't that exciting!"

Tilly nodded and smiled, then allowed herself to be led out of the station to the car park.

"How was your journey, sweetheart? You look a bit dazed – did you fall asleep? I always feel sleepy on trains, it's the way they rock from side to side."

"I was asleep," Tilly admitted. "I set my phone alarm, though. I wouldn't have missed the stop."

"No, I'm sure you were very careful. Come on, in you get. Did you open your great-gran's parcel on the train? She had me up in the attic searching everywhere for the photo albums and that box of old-fashioned decorations."

Tilly blinked, remembering. Of course – Lucy's beautiful decorations. The golden basket with the bright red roses. She pulled it out of her coat pocket and sat staring at it on her lap. "Yes," she muttered huskily to Grandma. "She said in her letter she'd tell me about it."

Grandma Ellen laughed. "She's got everything out to show you." She glanced over at Tilly. "I think it's been good for her, actually. She hasn't thought about all those stories in so long."

They bumped along the narrow lane towards Grandma and Great-Gran's cottage, and Tilly peered at the fields and the hills rising up in the distance. The farmhouse was over there, where her cousins lived. Just at the foot of that hill. Her uncle Matt ran the farm now. Was it the same farmhouse? Would she recognize it? Uncle Matt and Auntie Rosie had changed the house around a lot but surely there would be something left, if she looked carefully. Tilly tried to remember how the bedrooms were laid out upstairs. She wondered what had happened to her patchwork quilt. Tilly shook her head, confused. She felt as if she was caught between two times and didn't belong in either.

"Here we are! And there's Great-Gran at the door to see you, Tilly. And Tarran. Goodness me."

A black-and-white sheepdog darted out of the door as Great-Gran opened it, arrowing towards Tilly as she clambered out of the car. She stared at him, her mouth falling a little open as he nuzzled lovingly at her hands. Then she crouched down, giggling as he licked her chin and sniffed her thoroughly all over.

It wasn't the same dog. Of course it wasn't. Tarran had been alive eighty years before. Great-Gran must have had many, many dogs since then. But she wasn't the same Tilly, either, and yet she had been there. She *had*.

"You're a hero," she whispered in Tarran's ear, as he frisked round her, his feathery coat brushing silky-soft against her hands. "You saved Mister and you saved me."

"He's being so friendly!" Grandma said, coming round the car with Tilly's bag. "What's got into him, Mum?" she said to Great-Gran, who was walking down the little front path, holding her cardigan tightly round her against the cold.

Tarran turned back and whisked himself twice round Great-Gran's feet and she rubbed the silken dome of his head, smiling down at him lovingly. Then she put her arm round Tilly's shoulders. "He's just pleased to see Tilly. I've been thinking about you so much, lovey."

"Me, too, Great-Gran." Tilly hugged her tight. "You wouldn't believe how much." She reached down to stroke Tarran's head, too, and he pressed himself between them, looking up at them both with those same shining dark eyes that Tilly remembered from so long ago.

"We should get out of this snow and into the warm," Great-Gran murmured. "The fire's lit. We've got some stories to tell you, Tarran and me."

Tilly nodded, winding her fingers into Great-Gran's. "Tell me every single one!"

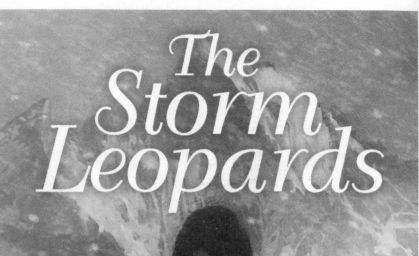

Collect them all!

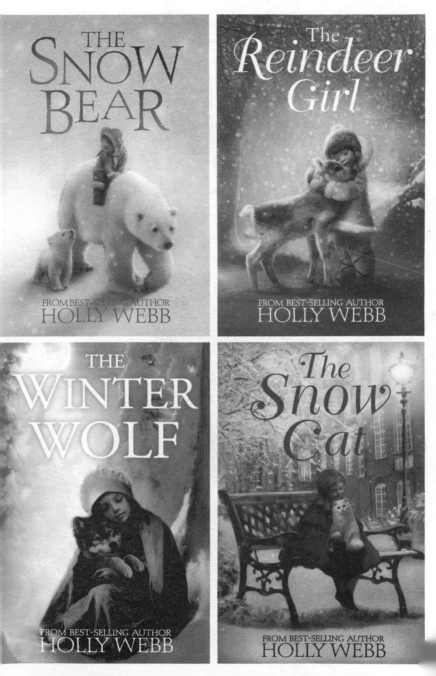

THE SNOW BEAR

FROM BEST-SELLING AUTHOR
HOLLY WEBB

The Reindeer Girl

FROM BEST-SELLING AUTHOR
HOLLY WEBB

THE WINTER WOLF

FROM BEST-SELLING AUTHOR
HOLLY WEBB

The Snow Cat

FROM BEST-SELLING AUTHOR
HOLLY WEBB

Also by HOLLY WEBB:

HOLLY WEBB

The HOUNDS of PENHALLOW HALL

THE MOONLIGHT STATUE

Illustrated by
JASON COCKCROFT

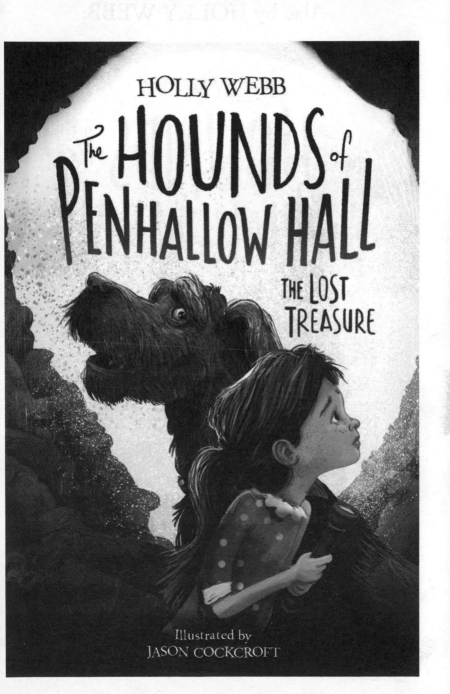

HOLLY WEBB

The HOUNDS of
PENHALLOW HALL

THE LOST
TREASURE

Illustrated by
JASON COCKCROFT

HOLLY WEBB

Holly Webb started out as a children's book editor, and wrote her first series for the publisher she worked for. She has been writing ever since, with over one hundred books to her name. Holly lives in Berkshire, with her husband and three young sons. Holly's pet cats are always nosying around when she is trying to type on her laptop.

For more information
about Holly Webb visit:

www.holly-webb.com